THE GIANT'S TOE

THE GIANT'S TOE

BROCK COLE

A *Sunburst Book* · *Farrar, Straus and Giroux*

For Zoë

Copyright © 1986 by Brock Cole
All rights reserved
Library of Congress catalog card number: 85-20569
Published in Canada by
Collins Publishers, Toronto
Printed in Singapore
First edition, 1986
Sunburst edition, 1988

Once there was a giant out hoeing in his cabbages.

The hoe slipped and he gave his foot a mighty whack.

"Ow!" he cried. "I must have cut off my toe."

But when he found his toe among the cabbage
leaves it had changed. It didn't look like a toe at
all.

Still, he thought he had better keep it, and he
put it in his lunch pail.

"I'll glue it back on," he said to himself.
"But no, I might want to take a bath someday, and
then it would come off. I'll sew it back on. But no,
that might prick…"

The giant muttered and hoed until he forgot all
about his toe.

After a while he began to get hungry, so he sat down and opened his lunch pail.

"Where's my pie?" he said.

"I ate it," said the toe.

"Toes don't eat pies," said the giant.

"I was hungry," said the toe.

"Hmph," said the giant. "You don't know how a toe ought to behave, and I'm going to do away with you."

"Oh, you think so," said the toe. "How are you going to do that?"

"I'm going to make you into a pie, that's how," said the giant.

And he made a pie and put the toe inside.

"Now," he said, "I'm going to get kindling for the fire."

No sooner had the giant stepped out of the kitchen than a greedy fat hen hopped up on the table and started pecking at the pie crust. Soon she had made a big hole.

Out popped the toe and pushed her inside.

When the giant came back, he built a big fire in the stove and put the pie in the oven. Soon a delicious aroma filled the air.

"Oh my, that smells good," he said. "Toe pie must be wonderful!"

While the giant muttered and rubbed his hands
and licked his lips, the toe set the table.

"What are you doing?" asked the giant.

"I'm helping," said the toe.

"But you're supposed to be in the pie!"

"I put a chicken in instead," said the toe.

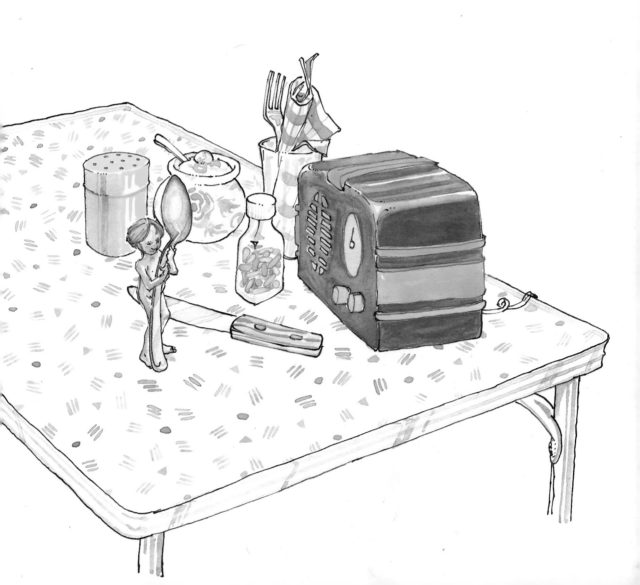

"What?" cried the giant. "That's my hen that lays the golden eggs!"

Oh, the giant was mad. When he saw that the pie was baked up all nice and brown, he broke three plates and a gravy boat.

When the giant calmed down, he and the toe ate the pie.

"Now, Toe," he said, "I'm really going to do away with you."

"Oh, you think so," said the toe. "And how are you going to do that?"

"You see this bag?" said the giant, putting a velvet bag on the table and taking out a golden harp. "I'm going to put you in this bag, and then I'm going to dig a hole all the way to China and throw you in, that's how!"

And he put the toe in the bag.

"Wait a minute," cried the toe. "It's so dark in here I couldn't find my nose if I had to blow it."

So the giant gave him a candle, just to keep him quiet, and went out in the garden to dig.

With the candle, the toe burned a hole in the bag big enough to squeeze out, and then he pushed the harp back inside.

When the giant finished his digging, he fetched the bag and threw it down to China.

"Be gone, foul Toe!" he cried, and then he quickly filled in the hole.

The toe helped him stamp down the dirt.

"What are you doing?" said the giant.

"I'm helping," said the toe.

"But you're supposed to be in the bag!"

"I put the harp in instead."

"But that was my golden harp that plays and sings all by herself!" bellowed the giant, and he stamped and tramped until the dust fairly flew.

"Oh, Toe!" he cried. "This time I'm really going to do away with you!"

Just then, there was a loud knocking at the gate.

"I'll get it," said the toe, and off he went before the giant could stop him.

"I'm Jack," said as mean-looking a boy as ever
was. "And I want the hen that lays the golden eggs."

"Too late," said the toe. "We ate her."

"Then where's the golden harp?" demanded Jack.

"Gone to China," said the toe.

"Then I'll chop up the giant!" bellowed Jack.

"Too late," said the toe. "He already chopped himself in two."

"He did?" said Jack.

"That's right," said the toe. "A big piece and a little piece."

When Jack heard that, he knew he was out of luck, so off he went to find some other giant.

"Well," said the giant when Jack was gone. "I suppose I'm the big piece and you're the little piece."

"That's right," said the toe.

"And I suppose I can't do away with you, after all," said the giant.

"No, you can't," said the toe.

"Hmph," said the giant. "Then I won't."

And he and his toe lived happily ever after, just as they should.